PORNADA

POR

Mary Francis Shura

MARY FRANCIS SHURA

pictures by Erwin Schachner

ATHENEUM   1970   NEW YORK

NADA

Best wishes to Jim.
Feb. 5, 1983,

Text copyright © 1968 by Mary Francis Shura
Pictures copyright © 1968 by Erwin Schachner
All Rights Reserved
Library of Congress catalog card number 68-18459
Published simultaneously in Canada
by McClelland & Stewart Ltd.
Manufactured in the United States of America
by Kingsport Press, Inc., Kingsport, Tennessee
Designed by Judith Lerner
First Printing July 1968
Second Printing August 1970

TO JACKIE THE GEM-FINDER
under the shadow of
Bishop's Cap

PORNADA

1

FRANCISCO could hear his friends calling him, but he did not answer. He kept his eyes shut, waiting for the boys to give up and go away. This was not a day to wander through the streets of Juarez or play baseball or even dive for pennies under the bridge. This was a green lizard day to slip from sleep to sunny wakefulness, wrapped in the humming quiet of a July afternoon.

"Maybe I am just lazy," he whispered to the sly lizard who stared at him from the yucca stalk. "But it is so good a world." His eyes were drifting shut again, slowly, slowly like a feather from a high hawk. "And so quiet," he added drowsily to the lizard.

But the lizard was gone, gone as quickly as the quiet!

Francisco sat up to look. The air was filled with squealing and grunting and yelling and the honking of many horns. The noise was as near to Francisco as the width of the Rio Grande which flowed bank full between him and the highway on the other side.

It took only one noisy minute to realize what had happened. A man in brown pants was yelling very loudly. The wooden slats in the back of his truck had broken out and pigs were rolling out of the truck like sausages. Pigs were everywhere, running along the river bank, squealing and grunting. Even though the man had pulled his truck off onto the strip of green along the road's side, the little pigs were running wildly onto the highway, so that cars from each direction squealed to a halt, honking their horns to pass.

Francisco stared in astonishment. No pig must ever walk on the great highway to El Paso!

Francisco kicked off his huaraches swiftly and plunged into the river, swimming as hard as he could. When he reached the other side, he shook

himself, called *"Buenos Días"* to the man in the brown pants, and began to chase the little pigs.

They ran very fast. Each time he caught one, it wriggled in his arms, with its small legs still running. One by one he brought them back to the man.

First he caught the ones in the road. *"Uno, dos, tres, cuatro, cinco, seis, siete,"* Francisco counted. With that there were no more pigs on the highway.

"Ocho, nueve, diez, once, doce," he went on. With that there were no more pigs on the broad bank between the highway fence and river.

"Trece, catorce, quince," Francisco finished, quite out of breath. Now no more pigs rooted happily along the muddy bank of the Rio Grande.

At least Francisco didn't see any.

The man looked at Francisco helplessly as he braced himself against the back of the truck. The pigs squealed so loudly from inside that Francisco had to lean very close to hear what the man was saying.

"Thank you, thank you, son," the man was shouting. "But what can I do now? The minute I let go, they will all be out and gone again."

"Un momento," Francisco replied. He climbed through the fence and ran quickly to the river. After a quick swim he was on the other side where his adobe home clung to the barren hill.

It was useless to look for boards; he knew his father had none, but he did find his father's hammer and a handful of nails, slightly bent but still usable. Never before had he tried to swim the Rio carrying anything. When he was across, still carrying the tools intact, he felt a little taller than he had going in.

Francisco braced all of his weight against the squealing pigs while the man hammered the nails straight against a stone. Even with many straight nails, it took a great hammering to fasten the boards tight enough.

When the job was all finished, Francisco and the man looked at each other. Then they both laughed. They were soaking wet and streaked with the mud of the river bank. They were both very hot and dirty . . . and suddenly friends.

"I certainly am grateful to you, young man," the stranger said, shaking Francisco's muddy hand with his own, which was streaked with dust.

"*Por nada*," Francisco said. "I am only glad that you got your fifteen pigs back safely."

"Fifteen?" the man asked quietly with a puzzled frown.

"Fifteen," Francisco repeated. "Are there more?"

Instead of answering, the man seemed suddenly to swell like a puff lizard. He began to shout with annoyance. "That one! Mark my words! It will be that one. That dreamer, that lazy one." He shouted so angrily that people passing in cars along the highway turned to stare at him.

"Then there were sixteen?" Francisco guessed.

The man nodded angrily. "I know which pig it must be. That dreamer! I can imagine him standing on his great ugly hind legs to look at the view, and breaking the slats of my truck. He thinks he is an artist, that pig."

Francisco looked carefully up and down the stream bank. "Where can the pig be?" he wondered out loud.

The man was wiping his hot arms with a huge red bandanna. "Watching the fishes, or staring at flowers . . . something foolish," he grunted.

Francisco stood thinking for only a minute. Then he ran down the bank to a place he knew well, a place where grew a great prickly pear, which bloomed scarlet in the riverbank sand. Sure enough, there by the bright flower a yellow pig sat staring, his snout tilted happily at an open blossom.

When Francisco caught the round body in his arms, the pig didn't even wriggle. He merely turned and stared at Francisco. Then he smiled.

The man was not smiling. "That is the one," he

said disgustedly as Francisco and the pig drew near.

Francisco liked the round feel of the pig against himself. (He liked the feel of the pig's warm thumping heart under his arm, but most of all he liked the way the pig kept smiling at him, not seeming to mind being carried at all.)

"Is he such a bad pig?" Francisco asked gently.

"Well, not bad, perhaps," the man admitted reluctantly. "It's just that, well . . . when the other pigs are rooting for food along the river bank, he only stands and looks."

"The Rio Grande is like a great yellow ribbon," Francisco said softly, for he too liked to stand and watch it unfold between its banks.

"And when the other pigs curl in the shadows of the stable to make fat," the man went on accusingly, "He wanders about and stares at mountains."

"The mountains are like great painted pots at sunset," Francisco said quietly, for he liked to watch the mountains change color too. He hugged the pig a little tighter.

"And at night," the man said sternly, "When the other pigs dream of yellow corn, what do you think this one does?"

"Perhaps he watches the moon climb past El Christo Ray," Francisco guessed with a smile, "Or the stars crown the Bishop's Cap."

"You are exactly like my pig," the man said reproachfully.

"*Muchas gracias*," Francisco answered, laughing.

"*Por nada*," the man replied with a grumble.

Then they both laughed again for they were friends. The round pig jiggled in Francisco's arms as he laughed.

"Enough," the man cried, wiping the gleam of laughter from his face. "I must get these small ones to market."

When he dug his hand into his pockets, Francisco heard the jingle of coins.

"I want no money," Francisco protested quickly. "I helped you because I liked doing it."

The coins stopped jingling and the man stared thoughtfully at him. Francisco felt that very tall feeling again. He knew the man was not keeping his money because he wanted to save it, but because he and Francisco were friends.

Then they both smiled again, like the shaking of hands.

"In that case, you must take this one," the man said firmly. "You must take him as a favor to me, your friend. Then the two of you can watch the ribbon of the river and the colors of the mountains and the Bishop's Cap with stars (I use your own words). This pig is for nothing . . . *Por nada!*"

"Oh, no sir, you musn't," Francisco protested. "Not a whole pig!"

The man's laughter rolled about them. "What use would I have for half a 'for nothing' pig like that, when I cannot even use a whole one?"

The man got into his truck too swiftly for argument. Dust swirled from his hind wheels. Francisco, with the pig tightly in his arms, ran after the truck to call, *"Gracias, Señor. Gracias. Mucho, mucho."*

The answer rolled back in laughter, *"Por nada!"*

2

THE PIG AND Francisco looked at each other as the dust settled about them on the highway.

"He has called you a for nothing pig," Francisco said gently.

The pig lowered his head and looked away.

"That will be your name," Francisco told him. "Just you and I will know better." Together they swam the Rio Grande and started up the hill to home.

Mama was standing in the open doorway, watching them approach. She was holding Francisco's little sister Josi in her arms.

"Mama, Josi," Francisco began to run and shout as soon as he saw them watching. "Look at my pig.

See my very own pig!"

"Your own pig?" Mama asked as if she could hardly believe his words.

Francisco was almost out of breath. Josi scrambled from Mama's arms to run and meet him. When Josi came to Pornada, the pig stopped running and stood very still. Josi stood still a moment too, then very gently she put her little brown hand between Pornada's ears and patted him.

Pornada looked at Francisco as if to ask if he could make friends with Josi. When Francisco smiled, Pornada walked along beside Josi, letting her hold him tightly about the neck.

Mama was smiling in her way. Always at her work, she hummed small pieces of songs and spoke amiably to the cooking pots when she thought no one was listening. But Francisco always knew that behind the darkness of her eyes lay tears that she tried very hard to keep from falling. Mama either smiled or frowned a little (which meant she did not understand) or scowled very fiercely, making her voice sound cross so that no one could tell how close she was to tears.

Now, since she was smiling, Francisco tried to

tell her the story so fast that she need not frown even once before she understood. "Pigs were spilling from a truck on the highway," he told her swiftly. "When I helped the man catch them and seal them in . . . he gave me Pornada—as a gift between friends."

"*Por nada?*" Mama frowned, still not wholly understanding. "What kind of a name is that?"

"It doesn't really suit him," Francisco assured her. "But since the man called him that, I thought I should use it for his name."

"It's not an ordinary name," Mama said, looking a little brighter.

"He is not an ordinary pig," Francisco said. "He is my own pig, forever."

"We will have to see what your papa says," Mama said doubtfully. She laid her hand gently on Francisco's shoulder for a moment, and then went back into the house.

Francisco stared after her a long moment with a sinking feeling. Why should Papa object to Pornada? Why should Mama even think of such a thing? Now there was nothing to do but wait until Papa came home. It would be silly to spoil the afternoon with worrying.

And such an afternoon of fun it was! Pornada was very curious. He explored the hillside about their home with Josi tagging along happily. When Pornada leaned over to inspect a busy anthill, Josi squatted on her short brown legs to stare soberly along with him.

Pornada even came into the dim cool house to investigate. When he saw Francisco's paintings hung along the wall, the yellow pig sat bolt upright on his small tail and looked at them with such pleasure that Mama stopped her work to laugh at him. Pornada sniffed at the blue vase of cactus

flowers that Francisco had arranged in the niche with the Madonna and found them beautiful too.

After Mama chased them all out of her way, Pornada lay in the shade of the chinaberry tree for a siesta. He didn't really sleep, but only lay watching the glinting river while Josi napped against his round side.

Francisco left them there to meet Papa on his way home from work.

Because of Mama's words, Francisco told the story of Pornada very carefully, watching his father's face with something like fear growing inside.

Papa listened without a change of expression. Only when Francisco was quite through did Papa speak quietly.

"A pig brings many pesos at market."

"But this is not just any pig, Papa!" Francisco protested. "He is an artist . . . even the stranger called him that."

"Is it not true that an artist pig eats corn like other pigs?"

Francisco's heart tumbled a little.

"And has need of a place to sleep?"

Francisco could find no answer.

"And will he not be taxed like other creatures?"

Francisco walked along silently. He watched the puffs of dust squirt about his huaraches and the wide fans of dirt that flew from under his father's larger shoes. Why had he forgotten that his papa was so practical a man?

Francisco looked up at his father thinking of how much he loved him. It sometimes seemed to Francisco that his papa had his mother's spirit turned inside out. For always behind his father's soberness there lay a brightness of laughter that could blossom within a moment.

Francisco sighed. There was this one place where he and his father disagreed. "It is better that a boy's hands learn work than play," his father reproached him when Francisco spent long hours painting with his brushes and paints.

The sigh was not lost on Papa. A little way from the house, he stopped. He tilted Francisco's head up so that he could see into his son's face.

"Do not think me heartless, Francisco, my son," he said gently. "But I am a practical man, and a poor man. We cannot afford to keep an artist pig."

Papa was right. Francisco knew that he was

right, but the rightness did not keep a hard knot from forming in Francisco's throat.

"But there is the money from my job!" he reminded Papa.

Papa walked on. "Soon school begins. You cannot sell chiles in the market during school. You spend your money now on paints and paper. Would you stop that foolishness for food for a pig?"

"I would for Pornada," Francisco insisted.

Papa sighed. "Until school begins, then," he agreed. "Then you will get rid of Pornada? It is agreed?"

The *gracias* he wanted to say stuck tight in Francisco's throat. Instead, he put his hand in his father's and walked along that way until they reached the brow of the last hill and Josi came flying into her papa's arms.

August came with a buttery moon and Francisco watched each day pass with a little sadness. Papa did not need to speak again of getting rid of Pornada, for he and Francisco had agreed as men of honor.

Every morning as before, Francisco raced the

sun to be at Miguel's stall in the market to begin his work. He called out clearly to the customers passing through the market. He described Miguel's vegetables in such glowing terms that sometimes Francisco saw Miguel's moustache quivering with laughter on his solemn face. Francisco sacked the chiles as swiftly as the wind, and ran home each evening with his coins swinging as a comfortable weight in his pocket.

Each night he counted his money into two equal piles. One stack of coins went into Papa's leather pouch and the other into Francisco's pocket.

But no matter how hard he worked, or how brightly he smiled, or how many centavos he brought home, they all went quickly to Rodriga the corn merchant. And still Pornada grew so lean that his ribs were a cage under Francisco's hand.

At night when the others were sleeping, Francisco and Pornada crept to the door and sat watching the line of moonlight on the river, as it waved and shattered and re-formed. Francisco stroked Pornada's lean body pressed against him. "I will find a way to buy you more corn, Pornada," he promised.

Pornada only smiled, wriggling his smooth snout
so that his eyes quite disappeared.

3

WHEN THE IDEA first came to Francisco he studied it carefully. He tried to think of all the objections that Miguel might offer. He determined that he would be very quiet and businesslike about his plan when he explained it to Miguel.

So one morning, Francisco made a special effort and got to the market before the birds left their nests in the supports about the market place. When Miguel arrived, he looked at Francisco with twinkling eyes.

"You have a look of festival today, Francisco," he said, beginning to unload his baskets. "What has you all excited?"

"Only a little idea," Francisco replied.

Miguel nodded. "Well, a little idea now and then doesn't cost a man much money."

"Oh, this is an idea to *make* money, not lose it," Francisco said swiftly. Suddenly his practiced speech was gone. He found himself waving his arms about with excitement and his words spilling out like beans from a broken bag.

"Think, Miguel, how miserably the *señoras* pant when they walk from market in this heat! Think how tired they get from chasing the children in the sun! Think how the chiles, (even your beautiful chiles) grow limp with heat on the long walk home."

"So?" Miguel asked, frowning the question at Francisco.

"So!" Francisco chattered excitedly. "Suppose I should take a little tray of chiles, covered for coolness with a watered cloth, and go to their houses. Would they not be happy to find me at their door? Would they not buy more chiles, perhaps even at a better price?"

Miguel chewed his lips thoughtfully, then stared at the sun, which was rising angry with heat, over the city. "We have nothing to lose but your footprints," he decided. "Let us give it a try."

That first day the *señoras* did not expect him so they did not buy too many chiles. The second day some were waiting for him. By Friday many depended on him. They even asked if he would add other things to his tray.

"I will give you an extra centavo," one *señora* promised. "If tomorrow you bring also *garbanzos* and two round red tomatoes."

The tray was heavier each day but so were the coins in Francisco's pockets. Even though the extra coins bought extra bags of corn for Pornada, still he did not grow fatter.

"That pig is leaner each day," Mama commented as Francisco and Pornada started off on an afternoon walk. "You burn his corn up on the roadway."

Francisco laughed. "Then it is a happy leanness, Mama, for he loves the mountains as much as I."

Pornada wriggled his snout sideways so that one eye winked in agreement. Francisco wanted to shout with pleasure. Instead he set off running with Pornada racing along behind him in his stiff-legged gait.

There were such good walks to take. They climbed to where scraggly trees strained for the very summit of the mountains.

Francisco would paint while Pornada sat patiently waiting. When his brush seemed to tire, they would begin to walk again. Even when Francisco was working at the market or making his rounds of houses with his tray of vegetables he would find himself grinning at the funny things that Pornada would do.

One day on the path Pornada found a strange dry pod. He grunted a question, then nudged the pod with his nose. It flipped and rattled as it fell. Pornada pulled back, then stared at it closely. Soon he began nudging it again and again along the dusty path. Francisco laughed at him, but when they reached home Josi was delighted. She seized the pod and shook it to make music while Francisco sat in the shade of the chinaberry tree finishing his picture.

Sometimes they walked around the mountains to where many houses clustered within neat gardens. Francisco felt that he and Pornada knew this country as well as the wind did. Surely they had

followed every path, and knew where the largest Devil's claws were and where each giant yucca grew.

And they made many friends.

Juan, the Potter, always greeted them with a wide smile, looking up from the vessel he held against the turning wheel. All about him in the sun his work was baking dry for the market.

Pornada looked at the bright pots with delight. He sniffed at each one as Juan and Francisco exchanged words of friendship. Suddenly a yellow bee flew crossly from the pot Pornada was admiring. The bee hummed narrowing circles about Pornada's head before it finally lit, stinging his tender ear.

Juan and Francisco both ran to help him but Pornada's fierce squealing continued until Juan pressed a little clump of cool wet clay to the sting.

"There," Juan said, "That clay will cure your pain."

Pornada ceased his squealing but he hung his head unhappily, the hurt ear almost trailing on the ground.

"What is the matter with him now?" Juan asked.

"I know that clay makes a sting feel better."

Francisco laughed. "I think he hangs his ear because it is not beautiful."

"Such vanity," Juan sighed, smiling. He looked about thoughtfully, then plucked a bright blue flower from a pot by the door. He pressed the stem of the flower into the wet clay on Pornada's ear. When Pornada lifted his head, the ear rose like a little flag. All that day, he wore his blue flower proudly.

They made friends with Donato, the Wood Carver. They both loved to sit and watch the great bulls form from the rough wood in Donato's hands. Francisco especially liked the friendly friars that Donato carved, and arranged in neat and studious rows until his next trip to the tourist market.

They met Manuel the Weaver, who made serapes like rainbows on a loom that complained with every movement of the shuttle.

But the friend they both loved the best was Guido, the Gem Finder, whose yard was overflowing with rocks and stones and tumbled treasures.

Francisco knew three things about Guido.

Guido knew more about gems than even the hills that hid them.

Guido loved money, for he worked very hard and dressed in fine clothing.

And Guido was lonely. He lived alone without wife or children, and when Pornada and Francisco came around the bend to his house, Guido would rise eagerly from his work to greet them.

"Welcome, welcome, welcome," he would cry as if no one word could hold all the pleasure he felt at seeing them. He treated them as honored guests, pouring fresh water into a low trench for Pornada and into a pottery cup for Francisco.

He would sit and watch them drink, leaning towards them with a smile. "What fine adventures did the two of you have today?" he would ask.

Francisco could tell Guido of each flower, what change there had been in the color of a mountain, and what scene he had last tried to bring to life on his paper.

After a while, Francisco began taking his new pictures to Guido who would spread them out in a line and study them one by one, sometimes nodding as if in approval, sometimes cocking his head to the side as if in doubt.

"In city shops I have seen many pictures that were not so fine," he told Francisco.

"The tongue of a friend is kind," Francisco smiled, not able to hide his pleasure.

Guido shook his head. "No, it is not that. In the houses of great men I have seen hung in costly frames, pictures that were not so fine," he insisted.

"The eyes of a friend see kindly," Francisco replied, but Guido's words filled him with pride. Words like these were his reward for the many times he sketched a branch over and over until the tree on the paper looked as if it could sway with the winds even as the real tree did.

"You are a rich young man," Guido would sigh, gathering the sketches together.

"I am happy," Francisco corrected him. "I have never one centavo to spare, but I have Pornada. I am poor like my father, but not so practical."

Soon Francisco had used the very last of the paper he had bought before Pornada came. Every sheet of paper had a picture on it, though there was still some paint left. Francisco looked at it and sighed. It would have been better if they had come out even. As long as he had paint left, he decided to turn the pictures over and paint on the other side.

Mama protested when Francisco took the pictures from the wall of their house. "What are you doing?" she asked, her smile disappearing into a worried frown.

"I will leave them if you wish," he told her hastily. "But . . ." Then he told her of his idea.

"Take them, my dear," she said quickly. "When they are double painted, they can be hung again."

Even Papa noticed how different the house was with the pictures gone. "How dark it seems," he said at dinner. "What has changed in this place?"

"The gold of the river is gone from our wall," Mama explained, "and the silver moon from El Christo Rey."

Papa glanced at the empty places where the pictures had been. He nodded, but said nothing.

4

Now that Francisco had only the backs of used paper to paint on, he grew more and more careful with his work. He felt he must not make the slightest error; each color must be exactly right, for soon his painting would be over. He knew how much he would regret any scene that did not please his eye.

It was not difficult to make the mountain paintings come out right. He and Pornada would simply walk to a place again and again until the painting looked just as Francisco wished it to.

But the paintings of Ciudad Juarez were harder to make perfect. The lovely secret alleys, the bright street scenes with puppet vendors and drowsy watchers, even the bridge that spanned the Rio

Grande, were hard to remember exactly right. Francisco would stand and stare, trying to hold each line in his mind until he could be home again with his brush in his hand.

"Perhaps I should take a painting or two with me," Francisco told Pornada, as he worked on a picture under the chinaberry tree. "Then I could look at the scene and know exactly where I was going wrong."

Pornada listened with his usual smiling attention. Francisco rubbed the pig's warm ear with his free hand. "You are a good counselor, Pornada," he said laughing.

Pornada only grunted and rolled over on his back in case Francisco might also want to rub his lean stomach.

The next day before leaving for the market, Francisco tucked three paintings carefully inside his shirt.

He meant to put them in a safer place but since Miguel was already setting out the vegetables, Francisco went to work at once. He began loading his trays, checking the list he had made the day before. "Three red onions for Señora Lopez," he was muttering, "two pounds of *garbanzos* . . ." Suddenly the pictures slipped and one fell onto the floor of the stall.

Miguel stopped his work to look at it, frowning. Then he wiped his hands and picked it up.

"This is from your brush?" he asked Francisco.

"It is nothing," Francisco said quickly. "Only some child's play." He thought of his father and wondered if Miguel might think less of him for playing with paints.

But Miguel seemed not to hear. Instead he stared curiously at the paintings, then began to nod quite amiably. "I know this place," he said almost with delight. "This is from the middle of the bridge looking that way . . ." he gestured with his hands.

Francisco waited, embarrassed.

"And you drew this!" Miguel said with delight, as if it were something extraordinary. "Maria, Jose," he called to his friends in the near stalls. "Come and see what this boy has done."

They gathered quickly and chattered with delight. Francisco did not know which way to turn from embarrassment.

"An artist," they cried. "Have you more?"

Slowly, Francisco pulled out the other two paintings.

The glassblower's wife seized one quickly. "Francisco, you must sell me this! Make a price. This is the place that my Manuel asked me to marry."

"It is indeed," Manuel said, smiling. "And with such a moon as that, too!"

"A real artist, this boy," Miguel boasted proudly. "Do not cheat him now."

Francisco solemnly accepted five centavos from Engracia and put them away. The coin felt different in his hands. He wished that he could keep it apart always because it was a special coin . . . the first coin ever to come from a painting. All that day as he walked between houses, he pressed the magic coin with his fingers and remembered the glow of Engracia's dark eyes as she bore his painting about the market to show her friends.

After that, Francisco always took pictures to market. He sold some of them from his tray of chiles. After his work with Miguel was through he showed his pictures in the streets. The tourists,

speaking with difficulty, asked him about the places and paid him fine prices for them.

This money he kept along with the five centavo piece that Engracia had first given him. He dared not count it, but only let it grow. When there were enough centavos, he could buy corn ahead for winter. Perhaps Pornada could stay. He said nothing of this at home. When school began would be plenty of time, and Francisco felt guilty about wanting to keep Pornada so much when he and his father had agreed as gentlemen.

Francisco's pot of money was heavy with money when August ended.

Two days before school was to begin, Francisco showed the pot of money to Papa.

"What is this?" Papa asked.

"Money left over from summer," Francisco said. "And Miguel wants paintings of mine to sell even when I am gone at school."

"So?" Papa waited.

"I thought perhaps . . ." The words did not come easily. He and Papa had agreed as men of honor. Now he was trying to change it. Francisco dropped his eyes.

Papa waited, saying nothing.

"Then Pornada must go?" Francisco asked.

His father nodded sadly. "I see no other way."

Suddenly Francisco felt his father's hand on his shoulder.

"What will you do, son?" he asked.

"There is the market," Francisco said slowly. "But I do not want to sell Pornada there." He paused. "I had thought of giving him to my friend Guido. He is fond of this pig too, and he is a lonely man."

"That would be very fine," Father agreed, looking a little more cheerful too. "That would be very, very fine," he repeated, almost happily.

Francisco and Pornada walked away from the adobe house and the ribbon river and into the hills.

All the way to Guido's house, Francisco practiced what he would say. "I must be practical like my father," he said soberly. "I cannot go to school and earn money for corn at the same time."

Pornada paused to listen. He nodded as if he approved of the speech, then trotted on, sniffing this way and that.

"I will give you my pig for your friend," Francisco practiced, hoping that when he was facing Guido his voice would not sound so near to tears.

Even from a distance Guido's house looked different. As Francisco drew near, he realized why. All the trays of gems had been taken inside and the dooryard was swept clean. A strange woman came to the door and greeted Francisco.

"I am watching these gems," she explained,

"while he is off in the mountains searching for jade."

"But when will he return?" Francisco asked.

She held her hands flat like a question. "Who knows?" she replied. "He said he would travel until he found the jade or gave up, whichever came first."

Francisco's heart was heavy going back down the hill.

At last the bend before his own house came into view, Francisco stopped. He kneeled down to take Pornada very close. Pornada did not understand but he held very still, only pressing his firm round jaws against Francisco.

Francisco could not even speak his thoughts aloud to Pornada. To think of the market made tears swell behind his eyes as if he were a tiny girl like Josi. If Papa only knew how much he loved Pornada! If he could just for one minute feel inside how it was with Francisco when the click of the small hooves and the cool snout announced that dawn was coming so that Francisco might rise and the two of them go together into the fresh of the morning.

"The very curl of your tail is dear to me, Pornada," Francisco said, his voice husky as if with cold. Pornada tilted his head, tickling Francisco's face with his ear.

Papa listened to the news of Guido's absence silently. He stared at the dust a long time before he spoke.

"Perhaps when Guido comes back," he said, "he will want Pornada. We might keep him until then for our friend. You could use the money that you showed me. When that is gone . . ." Papa's voice trailed off like a wisp of smoke into evening air.

When Francisco tried to thank his father, the words tumbled out so fast and breathlessly that Papa nudged him playfully.

"Enough words," he said. "Go and help your mother with Josi."

5

WINTER CAME with a suddenness like anger. It seemed to Francisco that overnight the wind turned chill and the sun lost its warmth. Although he wore more and more clothing on the mountain to paint and walking to school, the wind was stronger than the threads of his garments. The chill in his bones made every minute away from the fire uncomfortable.

"This will not last," Mama assured him, spooning extra hot *frijoles* onto his plate. "This weather is too cold to last!"

But Mama was wrong. Water froze, breaking a pot left out of doors, the brush withered and the cry of the wind was like an animal wailing.

Josi grew fretful from staying inside too much. She would not venture from the fire to play unless Pornada were with her, warming her with his broad warm side.

Although Mama went about her work wrapped in a great bright serape, she still hummed her little songs as she worked.

Now that he must spend all day at school and the twilight came more quickly, Francisco could only paint in the morning very early. Sometimes Francisco snuggled tightly in his bed, dreading the cold of the trip up the mountain.

At first he told himself that it was only the cold that he dreaded, but there was finally a time that he had to admit, even to himself, that he was afraid.

Morning after morning as he worked with Pornada eager and attentive beside him, Francisco had an eery feeling that a pale shadow moved where no wind could have stirred.

No matter how quickly he looked, he could see nothing, but still he was haunted by a feeling of being watched.

Just to be sure, he made a habit of piling smooth stones beside him as he painted . . . just in case.

Lying in bed, he thought of that shadow and dreaded to go into the dawn.

But Pornada would stand by his bed, his moist nose tilted at him, waiting. When they tiptoed from the house and shivered off to paint, Francisco made sure that Pornada walked very near.

The paintings of winter were different. Francisco used more blues and greens than ever before. They were chill paintings shivered with slender ice, the mist becoming a smoky blue against the frozen sky.

Although there were fewer tourists than usual because of the cold, the ones who came seemed to like these paintings as well as the others. Francisco was glad for there seemed to be more need for money than ever before. The fire in the corner fireplace had to be kept blazing day and night, and everyone was hungrier from fighting the push of the cold wind.

"I worry about you, Francisco," Mama told him, "walking in the cold of dawn. Could you not paint some other time, when the earth is warmer?"

Francisco laughed. "I cannot remember the warm anymore, Mama," he said. "So how can I wait for a dream to come back?"

Painting in the gray chill, Francisco thought of what she had said. If she knew about the unseen creature that seemed to watch him and Pornada, she would simply not let him go. He was very careful not to mention the frightening feeling that came almost every morning now. But always he kept a smooth stone handy.

All the brush and wood was gone from about the house so each morning as they walked back home, Francisco searched for fallen branches and small logs that would fit the fireplace. By the time they returned to breakfast they would come loaded like two donkeys, prickly with sticks.

"That pig is a wonder," Mama laughed, watching Pornada march in bearing a great bundle of faggots. "He is friend to you, bed warmer to Josi and even a burro for our firewood."

"And an artist, Mama," Francisco reminded her.

She took his face in her hand and looked at him a long minute, not smiling. "So much you love your pig, Francisco. I am half glad that Guido has not returned."

One morning when she was helping him unload

46

the wood, she noticed the large rock he still carried in his hand.

"What is that for?" she asked curiously, taking it from him.

He shrugged, not wishing to tell her a lie. "Isn't it a fine stone?" he replied.

"I shall warm it in the fire and put it by your papa's feet tonight," she said thoughtfully. "Perhaps that will help."

Francisco was relieved that she did not ask more about his stone, but the next day he found another to keep by him.

It seemed to Francisco that the cold wind was blowing all happiness from his mother. Each week she was quieter and smiled less. One evening he was watching her roll *tortillas* on the *metate,* her eyes downcast and her mouth sad.

"Are you all right, Mama?" he asked quietly.

She nodded without meeting his eyes, only keeping the smooth rhythm of her rolling.

Half shyly, Francisco went on. "If you have a worry, Mama, I can perhaps help."

She shook her head slowly. "No one can help," she sighed. "It is the cold. Papa . . . ," she began.

"Papa is not sick?" Francisco asked quickly. He felt very guilty. He had talked very little with Papa lately. Always when Papa came from work, he was too tired. Sometimes he fell asleep after supper before Francisco had even finished his homework.

Mama shook her head again. "Not sick, really, just the cold," she explained. "He needs more warm food and woolen clothes."

"I could take Pornada to market, Mama," Francisco said in a whisper, lest Pornada and Josi hear him.

She shook her head. "We will wait yet a little while," she said. "I know your love for Pornada. Maybe the warmth will return, or Guido come back."

Francisco rose earlier and earlier. He felt he must paint every picture he possibly could.

"That scene of the great rocks and the rising mist," Miguel said to him. "It is everybody's favorite."

"It is Pornada's favorite too," Francisco thought, smiling. He did not talk of his pig to Miguel. Who would understand how good a friend a pig could be?

The stony place where the mists rose had always been a favorite with Francisco too. The stones were great and gray and solid. The mist rising from the crevices in the rock was a thin delicate plume, wavering gently in the air, as graceful as a feather. The stony place had always seemed safe and friendly to him, but lately no matter how hard he worked, he always felt that something alien had come to this place. He kept imagining, just beyond his eyes, something lurking, watching them.

The extra new paintings of the rock and the mist and the pictures from the wall of the house made a great stack. Miguel took them from Francisco with a happy smile. "These will sell very quickly," he assured Francisco. "You will see!"

Only two weeks after he had talked with Mama, Francisco handed her a piece of paper money.

She turned it in her hands in amazement, looking at the lovely girl with flowers on her hair and a silver chain.

"Five pesos, Francisco. So much money!"

"For warm clothes for Papa," he explained. "I have done extra paintings so this is *extra* money."

She sighed, then drew him very close. "But you

no longer divide the money, Francisco. I see what you do. You buy some corn and a little paint and paper and all the rest goes for our food and fuel."

"We are lucky to be able to," Francisco said. "Pornada and I."

Papa seemed brighter when he wore the heavier woolen clothes. Josi ate her *atole* and played happily by the fire, but the house seemed very dark with the pictures gone.

Papa never mentioned them to Francisco, but one night as Francisco lay in his bed he heard Papa say wistfully,

"I miss the golden river that used to be there on the wall. I miss the full moon that lit this room when night outside had only darkness."

"Spring will come with the new moon," he heard Mama say hopefully.

The sky was still empty of moon the dawn that Francisco first really saw the wolf.

He and Pornada were sitting as usual on the mountain with only the pale light of chill dawn about them. The movement among the rocks could not be a mistake! Pornada heard it too, for he grunted. Francisco felt the pig's shoulder tighten against him. Francisco looked up. There on the ledge to his right a lean gray wolf was framed against the sky, his teeth bared, his legs tensed to leap.

Francisco seized a stone from his pile and hurled it at the wolf. The animal dodged it, then leaped for them, scattering the paints over the rocks. Pornada squealed fiercely as Francisco filled both hands with stones.

The wolf was desperate with hunger. Instead of fleeing, he came towards them slowly, seeming to watch them both with narrow gleaming eyes.

Francisco hurled stone after stone but the wolf only dodged and snarled.

When the wolf lunged, it went at Pornada, who seemed to turn into a flailing circle of sharp hooves. Just as the wolf snapped for Pornada, Francisco seized a great club of wood and brought it down hard on the creature's head again and again. The wolf finally fell limp on the rock between them.

Francisco did not even pick up his paints. He only seized Pornada and held his firm hard body tightly, saying the pig's name over and over to keep himself from crying.

Instead of faggots, they carried the body of the wolf to the road and left it there. Someone would come and take it for the pelt or bounty. Francisco did not dare take it home lest it worry his parents, but he was very proud.

"I am a mighty hunter," he shouted to Pornada and the mountain air. All the way home he sang loud songs of triumph into the rising day.

The very next night the new moon rose in a slim melon slice of light. That day the sun buttered the hill with warmth. By afternoon Josi was playing outside under the chinaberry tree, and Mama was smiling with her hand up as Francisco approached from school.

"Listen," she cried excitedly. Sure enough, above the sound of the river, came the low fluting song of a bird.

"We will have spring," Mama said so gaily that Pornada squealed as if to share her joy.

That evening she handed Papa some extra centavos.

"We have survived this bitter winter with gratitude," she said. "Would you buy some fresh flowers for the Madonna in our niche?"

Papa hesitated. "It would be more fitting for Francisco to paint a stalk of yucca like the Lord's candle for that place. Real flowers fade but not his painting."

Francisco heard his father's words with pride, and he wondered at these words from a practical man who wished his son's hands to turn to work instead of "playing" with paints.

6

AFTER THE bitterness of winter, spring was almost too beautiful to believe. As if by magic, the hills were flooded with color and the air heavy with the scent of growing things.

Each evening Francisco would race home from school to have more time in the hills with Pornada. Sometimes they took Josi who loved to go even though she found it hard to keep up on her short legs.

On one such evening, they were returning home for supper. Josi had chased every butterfly and examined every anthill on the mountain. At last she grew so tired that she insisted that Pornada *wanted* to carry her. Down the hill they went with Josi bobbing along happily on Pornada's back.

Francisco and Pornada stopped suddenly. Josi squealed and seized Pornada's ears to keep from being thrown off.

Down the road, walking along with a stick, was a tall man in a dusty robe.

"Guido," Francisco cried, "Guido, my friend." Off he ran towards Guido with Pornada racing stiff-legged behind him. Josi bounced along merrily hanging onto Pornada's ears and howling, "Halt, Stop, Halt" at the top of her lungs.

Guido looked up the trail at them. His face changed quickly from sadness into a smile and then into a shout of laughter. With swift strides he came to them and lifted poor Josi from Pornada's back. He smoothed her hair and hugged her, still laughing.

"Was that a ride, my little one?" he cried. "You are the Queen of the Caballeros, little Josi."

Although she had been near tears she began to giggle too, as Guido leaned to scratch Pornada's ears and then whack Francisco on the shoulder with his free hand.

"Welcome, welcome back, Guido . . ." Fran-

cisco said, jumping with pleasure. "How we have missed you." Pornada sat up straight on his back legs as if to remark how beautiful a sight it is to have a friend come home.

"Come for supper," Francisco pleaded. "Mama and Papa would be so proud."

Although Guido protested, they managed to get him down the hill. Mama and Papa, watching from the doorway, welcomed him in for the *enchiladas* whose fragrance spiced the air about the house.

"I am poor company, I fear," Guido protested.

"You must tell us over hot food," Papa insisted.

Papa's dinner prayer gave thanks for Guido's safe return as Francisco nodded happy agreement.

"You have traveled a long time, Guido the Gem-Finder," Francisco said as Papa served the plates.

"Perhaps you should call me just 'Guido' now," his friend sighed. "In all those travels I did not find the gem I was seeking."

"Was it jade you were seeking?" Francisco asked.

Guido nodded. "From a great merchant in Mexico City I got an order for all the jade I could bring him. So many miles I have traveled, so many banditoes I have seen fade like shadows behind the rocks of the hills, so many matadors I have passed on their way to battle." He sighed again.

"But no jade?" Mama asked sympathetically.

Guido shook his head. "And I was so sure that for once an ancient legend would be true!"

"There is then a legend about this jade?" Papa asked.

Guido laughed. "Such a legend. As a practical man I should have scoffed at it long ago, but instead I believed. They say that where jade lies sleeping under the earth a mist rises at dawn . . . that it is the jade itself breathing through the crevices of stone. Only artists and dreamers would believe such a tale, but I believed. In rain and sun I have searched every dawn . . . and still my hands are empty."

"You are like our Francisco," Mama laughed. "He too is a worker at dawn but he comes back with hands filled with paintings and faggots and great smooth stones."

"He is a fortunate young man," Guido sighed.

"But what great sights your eyes must have seen," Papa said thoughtfully.

"Indeed they did," Guido agreed. "I have visited the caves of the Indians whose turbans and serapes flower the dark hills, I walked through the beautiful city of the baldheaded dogs, and bought opals with hearts of fire in Querétaro."

"And music?" Mama asked. "Were there many Mariachis along the roads?"

Guido nodded, "Wanderers like myself. We shared many fires which fell to ash while their guitars played softly."

"But never," Francisco asked unbelieving, "never once did you see the stones breathe at dawn?"

"Not once in all these moons, my small friend," Guido replied sadly.

Francisco winked at Pornada. Should he tell Guido what he knew? But perhaps he was wrong. Perhaps it would be better to show him. Then he would know if these were the right mists.

"Enough of my troubles," Guido said. "Tell me how you fared through this bitterest of winters?"

"We have been fine," Papa said humbly. "And much because of Francisco. He has worked like a man in his boy's way, helping us through the misery of winter."

"No school?" Guido asked, alarmed.

"School too," Papa assured him. "But along with school, he has painted many pictures and with the money bought food and warm clothing for us and fed Pornada," he added smiling. He nodded towards Pornada who looked away as if embarrassed by the attention.

"Such a young artist," Guido said, "How are the pictures going?"

Instead of answering, Francisco went to the shelf where he kept the new pictures ready for Miguel. Very carefully he selected one to bring to the table. Guido looked at it, and then leaned nearer as if to see better. His eyes widened and he seemed almost frightened.

"Francisco?" he asked in a fierce whisper.

Francisco nodded, "What do you think?"

"This is true?" Guido pressed. "This is not a dream you have had, but something you have seen?"

Papa and Mama came from their places to stare over Guido's shoulder. Even little Josi pressed against Guido's knee for a better view.

"It is a nice picture," Papa conceded with a puzzled tone. "A tree whose leaves have left for winter, a hillside, and some stones."

"And mist," Guido cried excitedly. "Mist breathing from the rock . . . Show me this stone, Francisco, and let us dig."

"Pornada will lead us there," Francisco laughed. "It is his favorite place because he likes mist the best of all. He would lead me there each dawn if I would let him."

After he and Josi were sent to bed, Francisco heard Guido talking with Mama and Papa for a long time. He could not hear their words, only the warm rhythm of friendship in their rising and falling tones.

Even after all were in bed Francisco knew that Guido was as excited as he was, for he could hear him turning on the pallet they had laid for him before the last glint of the supper fire.

7

How SLOWLY the night passed for Francisco. Again and again he stirred with excitement. When he dreamed, his head was bright with the tales that Guido had told, and through them all rose the pale dawn mists of that rocky place.

Just before the day's first light, Francisco, Pornada, and Guido set forth winding up the rocky hillside. The trip was slower than usual. Although Francisco and Pornada knew the path by every stone, Guido needed to set his feet carefully to keep his balance on the rough trail in the half dark.

Sleepy birds stirred in the trees about them. An owl dived in whispering brush, seeking the night creatures who fed on the plateaus.

Then they were there. The three of them stood silent in the rocky clearing . . . when a gentle rose light stained the mountain, from the rock beneath the barren tree a small wistful finger of mist rose, wavering back and forth like a shy child uncertain where to turn.

Guido swung his pick in great circles. His shovel scraped and flung the earth back. He knelt on his knees, giving a cry of such gladness that Pornada, who was known as a silent pig, snorted with joy too.

"It is not very pretty," Francisco said with hesitation, as he and Pornada stared at the dark earth-stained mass in Guido's hand.

"Wait until it is clean and polished, my friend."

Dawn turned to day as they made their way down the mountain. Guido would not let Francisco help carry the jade. He had flung it over his back in a great brown bag. He sang loudly and a little off key as they strode down the path and into the doorway where Mama and Papa were getting ready for their day's work.

"Artists and dreamers," Guido roared. "They are the real gem-finders."

"I am so happy for you," Mama said, with her broad slow smile. "You will be as rich as you are happy."

"We will *all* be rich," he corrected her. "Half of this belongs to my friend here." He laid a hand on Francisco's shoulder with pride.

"It was Pornada," Francisco said.

"Pornada indeed. This is then the richest for-nothing pig in all Mexico!"

By that night Guido had polished a small piece of jade to a luster like a pecan leaf. Papa turned it in his hand with wonder.

"I decided something this winter past," Papa said with hesitation. "Work days end in sleep and dreams come. It is the same with being practical. There is a time for dreamers and artists, too. Is this not so?"

Guido nodded gravely.

Papa went on solemnly. "I am a practical man and a poor man. I cannot afford a lazy son. If painting is to be his life, he must work at this too."

Francisco and Mama were both staring at Papa now.

"Without Francisco's pictures," Papa explained, "we could not have survived this bitter winter. From now on, he must save his money for better things than food and clothes."

"Better things?" Guido asked.

"It must surely take many pesos to go to art school," Papa explained. "We must all help him. Even you, Pornada . . ." Pornada grunted with alarm to be addressed so sternly.

"You must take a wife, and raise small pigs for market," Papa explained.

Perhaps Francisco imagined that Pornada

blushed as he looked at Papa through half-closed eyelashes.

After Guido had gone home, Francisco fell asleep watching Pornada, who leaned contentedly against the open doorsill, making shadow pictures with his ears in the clear moonlight.

The next morning Mama looked at Josi playing under the chinaberry tree with Pornada. She looked at a piece of gleaming jade that Guido had left on the shelf. She looked at Francisco and his broad smile of contentment. Francisco thought she might laugh but strangely enough, she looked suddenly very cross.

"Such a shame," her voice sounded very angry. "The name of this pig . . . Pornada, indeed. This is a pig of our great fortune! Look at him. He is as slender as a snake. Pornada, you must eat." She flew at her pots as if they were enemies. She banged and stewed and fried until everyone fled the house.

But what a feast she made! She took her longest pan and lined up all the delicious things that she knew how to cook.

There were *tacos* with sizzling meat, *tamales*

rolled like blankets and golden with juices. There were *enchiladas,* then *chiles rellenos* and *frijoles* chocolate brown at both ends of the plate. Mama arranged this dish so beautifully that she admired it herself before setting it down for Pornada.

Pornada's hooves made a quick patter as he came. His nose twisted with beautiful smells.

Right in front of his wonderful feast, he stopped. He sat up with his nose tilted and his front paws just touching.

"Pornada, what is wrong? Why don't you eat?" Mama asked. Francisco could tell that her heart was almost broken. There was not a clean pan anywhere, yet this pig turned up his nose at her excellent food!

Josi came running to see what was wrong.

She hugged Pornada. "See the good food, Pornada," she begged. "Eat and be happy."

But Pornada only looked, swaying on his curled tail.

Suddenly Francisco understood. He came laughing to where Mama kept the large spoons.

"Mama, Josi, don't you see? It is too beautiful to eat!"

Francisco stirred the plate, while Mama wailed at the mess he was making.

"Now, Pornada," Francisco said, putting the spoon aside.

Pornada ate. He grunted with pleasure and winked from the deliciousness of it. He swelled with food so that even his ribs disappeared. Francisco watched while happiness rose in him like mists along the Rio on a night of chill.